MY FRIEND, BOOTS

by Leonore Ginsberg
illustrated by Tim Jones

Orlando Boston Dallas Chicago San Diego

Visit *The Learning Site!*
www.harcourtschool.com

Boots is my new pet.
We are friends.

As a puppy, Boots stayed with Beth Smith.

Beth Smith fed Boots.
She fed her well.

Beth put Boots in the bath.

Boots is a good dog.
I could use her help.

I met Beth Smith. "Here is Boots," she said.

Boots sniffed my hand.
Then she licked it.

Beth cried. I could see that she was sad.

I said, “Thank you, Beth.
Boots will miss you.”

I go to class every day.
My new dog is with me.

I think Boots is very special.